The Merry Wheels on the Bus

by **J. Elizabeth Mills**   illustrated by **Ben Whitehouse**

Cartwheel Books
An imprint of Scholastic Inc.
New York

To children's librarians everywhere —
Thank you for guiding children on storytelling journeys
that build imaginations and change lives! –J.E.M.

For my two twinkly stars, Yvonne and Timmy. –B.W.

Text copyright © 2024 by J. Elizabeth Mills
Illustrations copyright © 2024 by Scholastic Inc.

All rights reserved. Published by Scholastic Inc., *Publishers since 1920*. SCHOLASTIC, CARTWHEEL BOOKS,
and associated logos are trademarks and/or registered trademarks of Scholastic Inc.

The publisher does not have any control over and does not assume any responsibility for author or third-party websites or their content.

No part of this publication may be reproduced, stored in a retrieval system, or transmitted in any form or by any means, electronic, mechanical,
photocopying, recording, or otherwise, without written permission of the publisher. For information regarding permission, write to Scholastic Inc.,
Attention: Permissions Department, 557 Broadway, New York, NY 10012.

This book is a work of fiction. Names, characters, places, and incidents are either the product of the author's imagination or are used fictitiously,
and any resemblance to actual persons, living or dead, business establishments, events, or locales is entirely coincidental.

Library of Congress Cataloging-in-Publication Data available

ISBN 978-1-339-03808-7

10 9 8 7 6 5 4 3 2 1   24 25 26 27 28

Designed by Phil Caminiti and Doan Buu
Printed in the U.S.A. 40
First edition, September 2024

The text type was set in Baskerville. The display type was set in Rum Raisin and Cookie Regular.
The illustrations were created digitally in Adobe Photoshop using a Wacom Cintiq.

One merry bus goes HO-HO-HO,
HO-HO-HO, HO-HO-HO.
One merry bus goes HO-HO-HO,
All through the snow.

Two twinkly lights go BLINK, BLINK, BLINK,
BLINK, BLINK, BLINK. BLINK, BLINK, BLINK.
Two twinkly lights go BLINK, BLINK, BLINK,
All through the snow.

Three silver skaters GLIDE and TWIRL,
GLIDE and TWIRL, GLIDE and TWIRL.
Three silver skaters GLIDE and TWIRL,
All through the snow.

Four minty wheels go ROUND and ROUND,
ROUND and ROUND, ROUND and ROUND.
Four minty wheels go ROUND and ROUND,
All through the snow.

Five sledding snowmen TIP THEIR HATS,
TIP THEIR HATS, TIP THEIR HATS.
Five sledding snowmen TIP THEIR HATS,
All through the snow.

Six jolly bakers SHARE SWEET TREATS,
SHARE SWEET TREATS, SHARE SWEET TREATS.
Six jolly bakers SHARE SWEET TREATS,
All through the snow.

Seven singing carolers FA-LA-LA,
FA-LA-LA, FA-LA-LA.
Seven singing carolers FA-LA-LA,
All through the snow.

Eight snowy reindeer STOMP THEIR HOOVES,
STOMP THEIR HOOVES, STOMP THEIR HOOVES.
Eight snowy reindeer STOMP THEIR HOOVES,
All through the snow.

Nine wooden toys go BEEP and VROOM,
BEEP and VROOM, BEEP and VROOM.
Nine wooden toys go BEEP and VROOM,
All through the snow.

Ten busy elves wrap SHINY GIFTS,
SHINY GIFTS, SHINY GIFTS.
Ten busy elves wrap SHINY GIFTS,
All through the snow.

One merry bus goes HO-HO-HO,
HO-HO-HO, HO-HO-HO.
One merry bus goes HO-HO-HO . . .

. . . on snowy Christmas Eve!